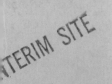

LIZARD TAILS
AND
CACTUS SPINES

LIZARD TAILS
AND
CACTUS SPINES

by Barbara Brenner

Photographs by Merritt S. Keasey III

Harper & Row, Publishers
New York, Evanston, San Francisco, London

*To Dodie, who got up so early
to go desert-watching with me.*

Contents

Writing a book is always, at least in part, a learning experience. In the case of this book I'd like to thank the following people who contributed either directly or indirectly to my education: Robert Craig, Arizona-Sonora Desert Museum; A. Gonzales, Organ Pipe National Monument; W. Hubert Earle, director, Desert Botanical Garden; George Foley, Herpetology Department, American Museum of Natural History; David Hulmes, New York Herpetological Society; Ernst Hoffmann, editor, *Herp*; Merritt Keasey III, writer and photographer of the Southwest.

And Cliff Harrison, desert guide and survival expert; Dodie and Dick Johnes, Arizona expediters and desert companions; and Stacey, Laura, and Karen Johnes, lizard spotters extraordinary.

1 Why Lizards?

My name is Alan Pippin (Pip for short). This book is about a summer that I spent in the Arizona desert, watching lizards.

Actually, I watched a lot more than that. I got to know plants and animals I'd never even heard of before. I learned how they survive in that strange environment. And I learned a little about human survival, too.

Still, it was the lizards that got me out there. So it's lizards that stand out most clearly in my mind. . . .

The trip wouldn't have happened at all if it weren't for my sister Jan. Jan is a botanist and she was working at a research station in Arizona. I wrote and asked her to let me come and visit, pleading my interest in lizards and promising all sorts of cooperation and good behavior, which we both knew I couldn't possibly deliver. But Jan invited me to come stay with her for the summer anyway.

My parents were agreeable, so I spent a month preparing. I read a dozen books on the desert, bought myself a pair of high boots and a water canteen, and begged six of my mother's old pillowcases to use as collecting bags.

My father helped me make a noose for catching lizards out of an old broom handle and some nylon fishing line. And my mother presented me with a great pocket thermometer for keeping records of desert temperatures. Because I planned to keep detailed scientific records. I wanted to write down where, when, and under what circumstances I saw each lizard. I had dreams of discovering a new species and of writing an article about it for some important scientific journal.

I arrived at the Phoenix airport on a hot day in the middle of June. Jan was waiting for me in "The Heap," her ancient army jeep. We collected all my luggage—tent, backpack, suitcases, and the empty fish tanks I'd brought for housing live specimens—and we drove out to Jan's place.

She was staying on the outskirts of the city in a house that had been built by a sculptor. He had designed it after the *hogans* the Navajo Indians build. It looked like two round igloos, if you can imagine igloos made out of adobe brick instead of ice. The two round parts seemed to grow out of the ground, and they were connected by a courtyard covered with a slatted roof. There was a little swimming pool in the back, open on all sides to the sun. By contrast, the houses were shady, dark, and cool. All over the roof of the courtyard hung bells of metal and clay. They rang softly when they caught the breeze, and each one made a different sound. It was the oddest house I had ever been in. And the nicest.

Jan and I spent our first evening catching up on family

4

gossip and eating the super vegetarian dinner she had cooked. It was after dinner that the lizard question came up.

"Why lizards?" she asked me.

What she meant was that of all the animal world, why had I focused on the saurians, suborder of the reptiles?

I laid out my reasons.

First of all, there's the fact that they're so ancient. Every time you look at a lizard, you're looking at a little piece of prehistory. Some lizards date back to the time of the dinosaurs. Both evolved from the same stem ancestors. The dinosaurs became extinct, but the lizards have prospered; they're found in almost every part of the world. When I look at a lizard, it's great to know that somewhere, three million years ago, a creature very much like it was running around.

I'm not alone in my attraction to lizards. Stories about them go back to the most ancient writings. Drawings and paintings of lizards can be seen among the oldest artifacts in the world.

But even if they didn't have such a long and impressive history, they'd still be a fascinating form of animal life. Consider the "typical" lizard. Four legs. Scales. Two eyes. A body with a backbone. A tail. Two chambers in the heart, five digits on each foot, two earholes to hear with, teeth, a tongue, and, in the case of the male lizard, two sexual organs called hemipenes. But that's only the most general picture of a saurian. There are over three thousand different species of lizards. And they can be tiny, large, fat,

5

skinny, speckled, checkered, striped, spotted, smooth, lumpy, warty, blotchy, spiny, shiny, iridescent, bright, drab, or able to change color!

Lizards reproduce by laying eggs. But some bear live young. Others incubate the eggs inside their bodies and lay them just before they hatch. And some species produce offspring from all-female populations!

Some lizards are legless. Some have a third, or *parietal*, eye, which may aid the lizard in controlling its body temperature. Some Indonesian lizards have "wings" with which they can glide for distances up to eighty feet. The basilisk lizard of the American tropics can run across the surface of the water. And most gecko species have toe pads which allow them to walk up a wall or upside down on a ceiling.

Many species of lizards can grow a new tail to replace a broken or lost one, and all lizards replace teeth as many times as is necessary.

There are a hundred other interesting ways of lizards. Some of them are unique to the saurians, others they share with all members of the class Reptilia. In any case, the lives of lizards have endless variety and color.

So, as I said to Jan, why *not* lizards?

2 The Place

It was Saturday. Jan wasn't working. We were going into the desert on our first full-scale lizard expedition.

I was ready and waiting at seven o'clock. Jan slowed me down, first by oversleeping, then by what I considered a lot of unnecessary dawdling and checking of supplies.

"Are we taking all this for a one-day trip?" I asked as I helped load the car.

That was when my sister gave me my first lecture on desert travel. You don't just go cruising out into the desert, I was informed. Those who do live to regret it. *If* they live. She was serious.

I watched her as she checked out The Heap. "This buggy is our only way out," she told me. "Not many people go where we're going, so you can't expect help from a friendly passerby. And there are no gas stations."

She checked the oil, gas, battery, radiator, tires, fan belt. She put an extra can of gas and a huge container of water in the back of the car. Then we filled our canteens with water. It seemed to me that with that amount of water we could have made our own river and *floated* to where

7

we were going. But Jan said it wasn't too much, and she proved to be right.

Next I was subjected to inspection. Jan approved my long pants and high boots, nixed my short-sleeved shirt and bare head. She said the more areas of your body you cover, the cooler you are in the desert. I changed to a long-sleeved shirt, and she gave me a broad-brimmed hat. At last we were ready to go.

In less than an hour we were deep in the desert. It was unreal. Like a foreign country, or another planet. Nothing was familiar. Where my eye was used to seeing tree-lined streets and shady woods, there were flat sunbaked roads and sand. There were almost no trees, and even the few we saw didn't look anything like our Connecticut maples and oaks and birches. We bounced along in The Heap, kicking up dust and watching mirages develop and disappear on the road in front of us.

We talked about deserts. Jan told me what defines them —water. A desert, she said, is a place where the rainfall doesn't exceed ten inches a year.

Water is the key to the desert. It even shapes it. Cuts out the canyons and rubs the stones smooth and cracks the mud and makes the little oases. It even shapes the plants and animals.

"You take desert plants," said Jan. "Out here the most important thing is for every organism to conserve water. Desert plants, like other plants, carry water in their stems and leaves. If they had big leaves, they'd lose a lot of water through evaporation. So they've developed small leaves. Or no leaves, like the cactus. And they have long roots

8

Plants in the Sonoran Desert

that reach down and get water from deep underground, or spread for long distances and soak up whatever rainwater falls onto the surface of the desert." Jan told me that some desert plants have roots that run for thirty or forty feet just below ground.

We talked for a while about how every living thing is shaped by the place in which it lives. Meanwhile, we were looking for a spot where we could observe wildlife—a place that was isolated but not too far from a road. We had a feeling that we'd know it when we came to it. And that's just about the way it happened.

We'd been driving around most of the morning, circling, doubling back, trying little dirt roads, when suddenly we came on it. A stretch of pure *National Geographic* desert. Full color. Rimmed by mountains, and looking really pretty under a June sun.

It was eleven o'clock in the morning. The sun was hot, bright, and fierce. It had come up from behind the mountains and taken over the whole sky. Under the sun were the mountains. They were high and farther away than they looked. It's colder up there in the mountains. The things which live in a desert may not be able to live in the mountains. The things which live up there may not survive down in the desert.

The spot we had picked was divided into two parts. On one side was a gentle slope called a *bajada*. It was covered with low-growing plants and tall Saguaro Cacti.

At the base of the bajada was a sandy flatland. Here the ground was hot and dry; everything was beige and tan and brown. Jan called off the names of the plants for me. *Bursage. Creosote. Mesquite. Cholla.* They were all pale desert colors. Even the cacti were pale green under that brutal sun. The only dark spots on the landscape were an occasional outcropping of lava rock and some areas where the ground was covered with flat stones made smooth by water. What the geologists call a desert pavement.

There was a dry streambed which separated the bajada from the flatland. An arroyo. It was about two feet deep and was cut into the earth in a clear path from the mountains.

There were trees along the banks of the arroyo—unfamiliar desert trees. *Paloverde. Acacia. Ironwood.* Jan knew them all. She said they were there to catch the water that sometimes ran down from the mountains and through the arroyo. Right now they drooped like hungry beggars. The arroyo was dry as a bone.

The road we had come on formed one side of the stretch of desert. It was a dirt road. When we came in, dust and powdered sand followed our car like a small cloud. We didn't see another car all the time we were there. I began to have a vague feeling that something was missing. I finally realized what it was.

"There's nothing here," I remember blurting out to Jan.

Jan didn't get my point at all. For her, there was plenty there. All kinds of low-growing plants and grasses, cacti, and bushes. She could have spent a year and still not investigated all the species of vegetation in that desert.

"I mean there are no *living* things," I amended.

She was annoyed. "What do you think plants are?"

"I mean where is everything? Where are all the animals? There aren't even any birds."

Jan tried to soothe my disappointment. "It's getting to

the hottest part of the day. This is when the birds go higher in the sky to catch the cooler currents of air. And you know the lizards go underground to cool off." I agreed that that was where they must be.

I guess the rodents and insects were underground, too. We certainly did see holes. There were holes of every size and description. They could have been holes of ants, beetle holes, badger and skunk holes, holes of the wood rat, or holes of the ground squirrel. But there didn't seem to be a single living creature on top of the ground.

"They could just be holes," I said skeptically. "Just breaks in the sand."

"Not on your life," said Jan. "Look here." She pointed to some droppings near a hole. They had obviously been made by a small animal.

I was somewhat cheered by the fact that there was evidence of something alive. On the other hand, I hadn't come three thousand miles to see rabbit pellets as the high spot of my day. I told Jan that. She laughed and said, "Patience isn't your long suit, Pip. But you'll have to learn to be patient in the desert or you won't see anything. Why don't we have some lunch and then come back."

While we ate and drank in the shade of The Heap, Jan explained to me that the desert requires a different kind of looking. "You have to learn to look *under* and *inside* and *overhead*," she said. "Your eye has to become attuned to tiny movements and to small differences in the contour of the ground. Try to separate colors to detect camouflage," she suggested. "Then you'll begin to see things."

After lunch we tried again. The first things we began to

see were birds' nests. Soon we began to see birds. The Cactus Wrens hung out in the cholla, and the Gila Woodpeckers popped in and out of holes in the Saguaro. An occasional hawk flew high over our heads, scouting mice and ground squirrels and lizards.

The hawk and I were having about the same luck with the lizards. By two o'clock I was sure there wasn't a single lizard in the whole Sonoran Desert. *The living desert, my foot*, I thought.

Then I saw it out of the corner of my eye. A small movement near where Jan was standing. It had been scrambling up out of the arroyo when Jan had moved and frightened it. It streaked past us and made for a bush. But not so fast that I didn't see its long tail and pointed snout, its tiny body and the stripes.

It stayed under the bush for a minute or two, then darted out again. I stood there, noose and pillowcase in hand, feeling foolish. That lizard had really moved. Noosing that baby was a joke. Another one of my dreams shattered.

"It's too bad, Pip," Jan said sympathetically as we walked back to the car. "You didn't catch anything. We'll have to get up earlier, I can see that."

But somehow I didn't feel disappointed. At least I had seen a lizard. And where there was one, there were bound to be more. After all, weren't lizards supposed to be the most plentiful desert animals?

I clutched my field guide happily and read aloud about the Western Whiptail. My first lizard.

3 The Life of the Whiptail

The Western Whiptail (*Cnemidophorus tigris*) is one of about twelve species of whiptails found in the United States.

I was to see a lot of the genus *Cnemidophorus* (pronounced Nem-i-DOF-or-us) before the summer was out. In fact, the "nemmies," as we got to call them, seemed to be almost everywhere we went.

Whiptails are all smooth-scaled, slim-bodied lizards, and they all have long tails. Some are striped (the Six-lined Racerunner), others are checkered (the Checkered Whiptail), and still others are spotted and mottled (like the Marbled Whiptail). Their pointy snouts are a good recognition feature; no other lizard has quite the long "nose" of the whiptail. No other lizard has quite so peculiar a life-style either. Among certain populations of whiptails, all of the lizards are female. They lay eggs and bear young without ever mating with a male.

We found "nemmies" among rocks, under bushes, and in sandy washes. Many times the sound of our footsteps would flush one out of hiding. It required instant looking to try to identify the species. The lizard would never oblige by

Western Whiptail Lizard

hanging around so I could get a better look. It would always scurry away at high speed, swooshing its tail back and forth in the way that has given it its name.

Sometimes one would let me get close before it dashed away under a bush. At other times our presence would send it dashing down any hole that was nearby. But after a while it got so I could catch the streak of a "nemmy" out of the corner of my eye and get a good look before it took off.

I tried to noose them at first. I noosed a lot of empty air before I realized that the only way to catch a whiptail is to pounce. Even then, your reflexes have to be in fine shape. After a while I got the hang of it. I'd throw myself on the ground like a runner sliding into home plate. Often, I'd come up with a whiptail in my hand.

It got so I could sometimes tell if one had been in the vicinity recently. I'd look for the tiny ripple in the sand that gives away where the tail has lashed back and forth. Jan complimented me on my increased powers of observation.

One day we both saw something too big to miss—a Roadrunner.

If you've never seen a Roadrunner, it's a shock. It's a huge bird, maybe two feet tall. The Roadrunner has solved the problem of getting food in an interesting way. Instead of flying around and coming down to feed like other birds, it *stays* down and runs around on the ground. That way it's always there in case a meal turns up. The Roadrunner's idea of a good meal is pretty broad. A typical day's menu could include a few slugs, a tarantula or two, a baby bird, a snake, and a few lizards.

16

The day we saw the Roadrunner, it was after a small whiptail. The lizard was crossing an open stretch of sand, which exposed it to the sharp eyes of the big bird.

The Roadrunner ran the whiptail down with incredible speed. It grabbed it in its long beak and ran with it to a rock. There it proceeded to slam the lizard against the rock until it was dead. When it was limp and lifeless, the Roadrunner gulped it down. It was still swallowing when its eyes began darting around, looking for the next meal. The Roadrunner has got to be Public Enemy Number One of small lizards.

After about a week at Jan's, I discovered that there were whiptails in her courtyard. They weren't wanderers from the desert; they lived there.

Lizards don't range very far from a home base. If a lizard travels more than a few hundred feet in its whole lifetime, it's a lot. So if you're a lizard, it's important to be born in a good spot. The whiptails in Jan's courtyard were lucky. The courtyard was sheltered from the hottest rays of the sun. There were lots of plants and plenty of food in the form of ants, beetles, spiders, and moths. There were no animals that could prey on them. And there was one other thing that made it an ideal home—plenty of water.

You could always find a whiptail around one of the outside faucets, catching the drips. They seemed to know where the faucets were and would visit them like people going to a drinking fountain. Each time the flowers were watered, we'd see a half dozen little whiptails in the ground cover, lapping water from the leaves with their tongues.

I started to make notes on where I saw certain ones, to

see if each individual had its territory. One in particular, a large Checkered Whiptail, seemed to hang around by the faucet outside my bedroom. But I had no way of knowing if I was seeing the same lizard there every day, or several look-alikes. I decided to mark it in some way.

So how do you mark a lizard? Do you band it like you band a bird? Can you put a dot of paint on it? I discarded the paint idea because I knew that color is one of the ways that male and female lizards recognize each other. I didn't want to foul up some lizard's sex life with a misplaced dot or two.

I went to the field guide for help. *A Field Guide to Western Reptiles and Amphibians* recommends marking lizards by snipping off a toe, front and back, on opposite sides of the body. I finally did it. It didn't seem to bother the lizard at all, but it bothered me.

I released the lizard and kept notes on where I had first seen it. Every time I saw it after that, I made a little map of where it was and measured the distance from where I'd seen it the previous time. I figured out that this whiptail seemed to live in a space about ten by twenty-five feet. That is, *I* never saw it anywhere else.

I began to think of "Two-toes," as I called it, as a pet. I tried to tame it. I'd put out a dish of dead moths and a small dish of water, hoping that it would come to feed. But I never saw it, or any other lizard, at those dishes. I guess they're attracted to live insects by their movement.

I thought perhaps handling it might make it more tame, so every time I saw Two-toes, I'd try to catch it. I didn't notice that the handling made it any more willing to

18

stay around or any more relaxed in my grasp. But it didn't seem any more scared than it had been, so I still had hopes. I kept thinking of the Belgian zoologist Rollinat. He trained Sand Lizards to take food from his fingers and to come out of their holes when he beat on a tin drum.

One day as I was handling the whiptail, the phone rang. I dropped the whiptail into a jar, intending to come right back. Somehow I forgot. About a half hour later I remembered the lizard. I rushed out to the courtyard. Two-toes was lying in the bottom of the jar, which stood in direct sunlight. The temperature inside that jar must have been 140 degrees. I didn't know how long it had been in the sun but I knew my lizard was in trouble. Like all reptiles, it had to move around from heat to cool, to keep its body temperature within safe limits. And I'd locked it in a container where it was literally cooking.

It took the lizard about an hour to recover. It took *me* a week to get over what I'd done. It was certainly a vivid demonstration of what it means for an organism to be *ectothermic* and have to depend on external sources to maintain its body temperature. Suddenly I felt lucky to be a mammal with an inner thermostat to keep me at 98.6°.

4 The Tail of the Iguana

I remember that particular day because it started with an argument.

"The deal was that I could go into the desert alone."

"After next week, Pip."

"But, Jan, I only *have* six weeks all together. I'll waste a whole week of exploring if you don't let me go."

Jan sighed. She had to go to work and felt that I wasn't quite ready to be on my own. I think she was beginning to feel that both lizard-watching and her little brother were a pain in the neck.

Finally we compromised. She would drop me off on her way to work and then pick me up on her lunch break. If it worked out, she'd let me stay all the next day by myself.

"I hope this is a good idea," she said dubiously as we got into the car. "It looks like today will be a scorcher."

I told her I didn't mind. I'd just wander around looking for lizards and not exert myself too much.

"You'd better be at this spot at twelve-thirty," Jan told me. I said I would and answered all her questions about whether I had enough water and whether I knew where the shady spots were and whether I would be careful. At last she was satisfied that I wasn't going to perish between eight and twelve-thirty. She left.

After the sound of Jan's car had faded, it was unbelievably quiet. Nice quiet. The sun was warm on my back, the sky was clear and blue, and I was just where I wanted to be.

I took Jan's advice—tried to sharpen my senses so that I could detect the messages of the desert. The first thing I noticed was the smell of resin. It was the creosote bushes. They were all around this particular strip of desert, and the air was filled with their pungent smell. I began to hear the birds, and then the softer hum of the grasshoppers and cicadas.

After my eyes got used to looking for them, I spotted some birds—a hawk of some kind and the ever-present Cactus Wren. I made some bird notes. Then I turned my attention to the ground. I saw a couple of ground squirrels. They didn't seem to mind running around in the heat. I watched them for a while until they ran off.

Two hours later the temperature was 104 degrees by my thermometer, and I was still looking.

About eleven o'clock, I noticed a shaking in the creosote bush near where I was standing. It was one of those movements that doesn't penetrate right away—you see a bush moving slightly in the breeze. . . .

And then I thought, *What breeze?* The air was as still as it can be in late morning on the desert. So what was making the bush shake that way?

It was a Desert Iguana! Big, with a handsome crest. I guess that, counting its tail, the iguana must have been well over a foot long. It was sitting near the top of the bush, displaying itself in the sun and getting a good view of the surrounding territory. It looked like an advertisement for lizards of the desert.

I figured it had been up there only a few minutes. I would have seen it if it had been there longer, even though its body was about the same dappled gray as the creosote bush. I also knew that Desert Iguanas are among the desert's late risers, because they plug up their burrows with sand when they bed down for the night. This keeps out the cold so well that they stay cozy until late in the morn-

Desert Iguana

ing. This iguana had probably just come out for a bite of breakfast.

Of all the lizards I could have seen on my first solo "watch," I guess the Desert Iguana was the most satisfying. It's one of the *diurnal* (day) lizards best adapted to the desert. These lizards have been known to stay out in the heat when most other desert animals have long since gone underground.

Now it was nibbling on a creosote leaf. Desert Iguanas eat mostly plants. They eat insects only if there are no buds or leaves around. I remembered they also eat their own body wastes, which seems to show a certain lack of sensitivity. But lizards are not particularly known for delicate feelings. Or any kind of feelings, for that matter. They seem to operate pretty strictly on instinct.

I moved. The lizard caught sight of me. It turned its head and looked me over sideways, slowly, the way some reptiles do. I could see its eyes clearly. They were large and the pupils were round, like all day-lizard pupils. It was plain that the lizard saw me. It seemed to be waiting to see what I would do. I stood as still as I could. It didn't move. Now it plucked another leaf from the creosote bush and chewed it, keeping its eye on me. I decided that it was a male, because its crest was so pronounced. I wondered whether there was a female around. It was egg-laying time. I thought of the possibility that there might be three to eight Desert Iguana eggs right under where I was standing!

I went back to admiring the iguana. That was when it occurred to me to catch him to show Jan. I figured to keep him in my catch bag until she came. Then, after she'd admired him and I'd written him up in my notebook, I'd let him go.

Of course, I should have tried it with my noose. Instead, on impulse, I made a lunge for him with my hand. Got him too. But only for a second. And then he had wriggled from my grasp. But not altogether. He had left me with eight inches of wiggly, scaly tail!

It's one thing to read about tail dropping. It's another to look down at yourself holding a still-squirming piece of lizard while the rest of him is streaking away across the sand on his hind legs like some baby allosaurus. The iguana had given up his tail for the safety of the rest of him.

I felt guilty and stupid. On the one hand, I knew that he would grow another tail, that I hadn't injured him permanently. On the other hand, I knew it would take a long time and that the iguana would be at a disadvantage for the time he didn't have his full tail. Lizards use their tails in a variety of ways. As a help in climbing, as a sort of balance, and as a defense. I thought of my own Green Iguana at home. If you come nearer to him than he likes you to be—he uses his tail as an effective whip.

I looked closely at the severed tail. It had broken off neatly. There was no blood. Instead, there was a small amount of colorless liquid, which looks like some sort of clear glue. That mysterious glue. Is that the substance that allows the lizard to grow a new tail? And how is it that a creature so much less complicated than we are can replace parts and we can't? And if we find out what is in that liquid, can we use it to grow new limbs?

I decided to keep the tail. I dropped it in my collecting bag. Just then, I heard the sound of a car. It was Jan, coming to get me.

I called to her as she pulled up.

"Have I got a *tale* for you!" I said.

5 The Horns of the Horned Lizard

We got into a pattern. Jan dropped me off in the desert early in the morning on her way to work. I met her at the highway in the evening. I spent the day watching and making notes on whatever I came across that seemed interesting enough to write about.

I'd learned a lot even in the two weeks since I'd come to the desert. I now "hibernated" during the hottest part of the day. I'd find myself a small tree or a ledge of rock and make myself a little shady lean-to with my tarpaulin. I also understood the principle that Jan had suggested to me that first day on the desert. More clothes is better than less when it comes to dressing for the desert. Now I brought an old sheet and took my afternoon siesta wrapped to the eyes like Lawrence of Arabia. The white reflected the heat, and the cover kept me from getting sunburned. I conserved my energy and kept cooler than the desert around me.

I was learning. I was also getting pretty good at catching the slower lizards with my homemade noose. In that split second when the lizard "froze," I'd slip the noose over its head and onto its neck. Then I'd jerk it upward, and often I'd have a lizard. I didn't keep them. I would just measure them, mark down the circumstances under which I'd caught them (time of day, location, etc.), and then I'd let them go.

We varied the pattern that particular morning. Jan had the day off, so she came with me. A lucky thing she did, as it turned out. Almost as soon as we got to the desert, she spotted something that I would have missed. It was a circle of bare sand with a neat ring of short grasses growing around it. The circle was slightly mounded in the middle and had a small hole in it.

"It's an anthill," Jan announced as soon as she saw it. "Harvester ants. They're the only southwestern ones I know something about, because they collect seeds.

"They have a whole granary under there," she told me. "The worker ants gather the seeds of grasses and carry them down to the storehouses where they keep them dry for food for the colony. They carry the empty seedpods up to the surface and dispose of them. See here," she said, pointing to the ring around the dirt circle, "here's where they put the discarded pods. But some of them still had seeds in them—that explains this grassy ring."

"Don't the seeds sprout under the ground?" I asked her.

"No. If they start to, the ants bite the seed heads off and stop them."

"Pretty clever." I reached out to pick up one of the ants as it emerged from the hole at the top of the mound.

"Don't!" Jan's voice was sharp and I pulled my finger away quickly.

"They sting," she said. "One bit me on the ankle once and I was limping for a whole day."

I sat back on my heels thoughtfully. Well. Stinging ants. Another feature of the desert.

As I sat there brooding, I noticed another mound. A little one under a prickly pear cactus. As I watched it, it began to move.

"Jan!" She saw it at the same time I did. A small shape separated itself from its gritty bed and came out into the white, hot light of morning.

It was a Regal Horned Lizard.

We watched it come slowly out of its sand burrow. It took about ten minutes. By the time it was fully in the sun, its color had changed from dark tan to light beige, which made it practically indistinguishable from the sand around it. It was the lizard's response to the sun—its color became lighter and would reflect the heat, as later in the cool of the evening it would become darker to absorb heat.

Now the lizard was all the way out of the sand. Even though I had seen pictures of horned lizards, I wasn't prepared for the strange look of it. Most lizards are longer than they're wide. This one was almost round. The tail was short, like a turtle's tail. And yet in some ways it resembled a toad—something in the shape of the head. We could see where it had gotten its nickname of "horny toad."

The body was a mottled, blotchy color. It was full of lumps, bumps, scales, blotches, fringes, and horny projections. The most curious ones were around the head—a ring of light, horny spikes, which gave it the look of a monster. But a mini-monster; the horned lizard was only about three and a half inches long.

28

Regal Horned Lizard

The lizard seemed totally unaware of our presence. It moved so slowly that I could have grabbed it with my hand. But I didn't want to. I wanted to watch it and see how it spent its morning.

In a few minutes it began to move toward the anthill. It took up a waiting position near the hole. We sat quietly, afraid that if we moved we'd send it scurrying. I got the feeling that the horned lizard had visited this spot many times before.

It waited at the entrance to the hill. In a few minutes the

ants began to come out. As they streamed from the hole, the horned lizard put out its tongue. It caught an ant and popped it into its mouth. Then another. And still another. Its aim was terrific and the surface of its tongue was sticky. Within a half hour the lizard had polished off a healthy breakfast. About sixty-five ants, by our count. The fact that they were stinging ants didn't seem to bother the horned lizard at all.

It stayed in the vicinity of the anthill for the rest of the morning. So did we. By noon our specimen had eaten about a hundred ants. Its belly was full and round.

Ours, on the other hand, were decidedly empty. And we were thirsty, besides. While we had been lizard-watching, the temperature had climbed to over 100 degrees.

We went back to the shade of the car to have lunch. It felt good to put my hands into the cool refrigerator that held our sandwiches.

After lunch we went back to look for the horned lizard, but it was gone. I guessed that it had burrowed to the cooler layers of sand under the surface to sleep out the hottest part of the day.

Jan said the worst thing she could think of was having to sleep in a bed of itchy, gritty sand. I remembered reading that horned lizards have valves on their nostrils which close when they go under the sand and seal off their nasal passages. Their bodies are designed like small shovels, with digging teeth around the edges, so they can get down under pretty fast. We agreed that if you have to spend a lot of your life in sand, you should be designed like a horned lizard. The horned lizard is really made for it.

Later that afternoon we stopped back at the spot where

we'd seen the Regal Horned Lizard. We had no trouble finding it. In fact, I almost stepped on it. This time it saw us.

A whiptail would have run. The horned lizard isn't much of a runner, so it has to make other arrangements for its defense. First it tried to dig into the sand and make itself as invisible as possible. I reached over and pulled it out of the sand and patted it.

It opened its mouth and made as if to bite me.

I patted it again.

This time it leaped into the air and flipped around sideways in a single motion.

I decided to pick it up and see if I could figure out whether it was male or female. Males have fatter tails and enlarged pores on the insides of their back legs. As soon as I picked it up, it began blowing itself up like a balloon. When this didn't succeed in terrifying me, it tried to jab me with its horns. I started to check out the back legs. It was then that the "horny toad" used its last defense. As I held it in my hand it began to hiss. At almost the same time I saw a drop of blood spurt from its eye and land on my hand.

I had read about this, but I certainly hadn't expected to see it. Even Raymond Ditmars, the famous herpetologist, handled hundreds of lizards before he saw one squirt blood from the gland at the base of its eyelid. No one is even sure why the lizard does it.

I didn't know *why*, but I certainly knew *what* had happened. I put *Phrynosoma solare* down and wiped the blood off my hands. We left it there, which was probably what it had wanted in the first place.

The next day we came out along the same road. As we

passed the spot where we had seen the horned lizard, we noticed several vultures circling overhead. That's usually a sign that something's dead, or dying. We stopped to take a look.

Almost on the spot where we'd been the previous day, there was the dead carcass of a king snake. Now, a dead snake isn't unusual in the desert. But this one was. It had two sharp objects protruding from its side. When I looked at them closely I recognized what they were. They were the horns of a horned lizard!

It was easy to figure out what had happened. The king snake had seen the horned lizard and, sensing a meal, had struck. A few seconds in that deadly hug and the horned lizard had suffocated. The snake had nudged it around with its nose and begun to swallow the lizard headfirst. It was then that the sharp horns had pierced the snake's gullet and come out its side. Now the vultures would eat both of them.

We were quiet going back to the car. Finally, more to break the silence than anything else, I said to Jan, "Horned lizards are protected in the state of Arizona."

"Only from people," Jan said. "Not from king snakes and vultures."

6 The Spines of the Cactus

I remember a day when, instead of looking for lizards, we hunted a cactus.

There were three of us that morning—Jan, her friend Cliff, and me. And some extra gear—Cliff's pistol and a rifle he'd stashed in the back of The Heap. I thought we were pretty heavily armed for a *plant*-hunting expedition. I said so to Jan when I could get her alone for a minute.

She shrugged. "He's a hunter," she said, by way of explanation.

I hoped Cliff wouldn't decide to pop off a jackrabbit or a ground squirrel while I was around. I don't think much of people shooting animals.

I had to admit, though, that Cliff knew his way around the desert. He brought us to a beautiful place. It's part of what is called the Arizona Uplands, and, though it's still considered desert, it has a completely different look.

At six o'clock on a June morning in the Arizona Uplands, the ground is damp with dew. The cacti look green and plump and juicy. There's a stream nearby that gurgles with water. The paloverde trees are covered with blossoms.

33

And the landscape is dotted with Saguaro Cacti. The Saguaro thrives in the Uplands. They're everywhere, stretching out their huge arms in those odd shapes that make them look like cartoon caricatures of people.

This is what Jan had come to see. She was doing a research project on the Saguaro. There were enough specimens on that stretch of Arizona Upland to gladden the heart of any botanist. She found a Saguaro of magnificent size. It was maybe forty feet tall and had more than a dozen branches. I thought Jan was going to throw her arms around it, which would have been a big mistake, considering that the Saguaro is covered from top to bottom with nasty spines.

After that morning on the Upland desert I understood more fully about ecosystems.

An ecosystem is a biological community of organisms that interact with the place where they live. The desert is an ecosystem. So is the Saguaro.

Start with a full-grown Saguaro. It stands in the desert like a big storage tank, getting its "food" from the water and nutrients in the ground. But at the same time that it's taking nourishment from the earth, the Saguaro is playing host to a variety of insects, which live along its stem. The insects live by eating little pieces of the cactus, and they in turn are eaten by larger insects. Which are eaten by lizards, mammals, and the birds that make their nests in the Saguaro. Like the Gilded Woodpecker and the Golden Flicker. They peck holes in the Saguaro and make their nests inside. When they leave, the holes seal themselves off, so the cactus won't lose any precious moisture. These

Saguaro country

Spines of the Saguaro Cactus

cavities become a permanent part of the Saguaro's structure. They are then used as homes by rats, mice, and Elf Owls.

But there's still more going on. Up on top of the Saguaro, where the flowers are, bees are feeding on the nectar of the waxy, white blossoms. So are white-winged doves and long-nosed bats. From the point of view of the Saguaro, the long-nosed bats are their most important visitors. It's the bats that carry most of the pollen from flower to flower. For a good reason. Saguaro flowers open at night, so they're more available to the nocturnal bats than to the birds and the bees.

Later in the season, the Saguaro forms fruit and seeds. The fruit is juicy and sweet and tastes something like watermelon. People eat it cooked or raw, and the seeds can be ground into a kind of "butter." Birds and other animals also eat the fruit. And the black seeds are eaten by mice and other rodents, which are in turn eaten by . . .

With all that eating going on, it's a wonder the Saguaro can survive. And a particular wonder that any parent Saguaro ever has an offspring that survives. Even if it does produce a seed that sprouts, how does a baby cactus combat drought and erosion? And what about cutworms, ants, and the rest of the nibbling, biting, chewing community of animals that feed on young plants?

It's not easy. Only one in twenty thousand Saguaro seeds lives to produce an adult Saguaro. Maybe that's why the Saguaro seems to have developed so many devices for survival.

Even the spines of a cactus have a purpose, Jan says. Not only do they keep some animals from nibbling, they also act like tiny fans. They break up the concentration of hot air and screen out some of the sun's direct rays. In fact, because of these odd little spines, a Saguaro Cactus can manage to keep itself about twenty percent cooler than the surrounding desert.

Cliff and I left Jan with her spiny prize and walked

toward the stream. We walked along a trail which had been worn down to bare dirt. Cliff said it was a watering trail used by animals going to drink at the stream.

As if to prove what he'd said, a jackrabbit hopped out of the bushes. It sat hunched in the path, twitching its ears like two antennae, picking up our sounds. I had never realized before how big a jackrabbit's ears are.

The jackrabbit decided that we were a presence that called for its departure. It hopped away. Cliff said that later in the day the jackrabbit would most likely dig a "form" in the sand under a bush and stay cool in it until evening.

I wondered why Cliff hadn't tried to shoot the rabbit, but I didn't want to remind him by asking. I asked if he'd ever seen any lizards in the Uplands. He said he had, but not this early in the morning.

It was getting warm and the water looked inviting, so we went in and splashed around for a while. Our clothes dried as soon as we came out.

I found the shed skin of a bull snake under a tree on the bank of the stream. We looked all over, but we couldn't find the snake. It's tantalizing to find the shed and not see the snake.

Later in the afternoon, after we'd eaten lunch, I wandered off by myself. I followed the river, then I went up the other side of the bank and out onto the plateau again.

In almost no time at all I managed to get myself lost. I couldn't find anything—car, road, stream, Cliff, Jan. I halloed hopefully, but no one answered.

I looked around, trying to get my bearings. Everything

looked depressingly the same. All cacti look alike, I discovered that afternoon.

I tried to remember something about the direction I had come from. I figured out which way west was by the position of the sun, but then I couldn't remember which direction the camp was. And why hadn't I taken my water canteen with me? Not too smart, any of it. I called again. Still no answer.

For some reason, I got really scared. I started to run around like a maniac. The more I ran the hotter and thirstier I got. And the Uplands can be just as hot as low desert. In about half an hour I'd worked myself into a sweaty state of near-hysteria. I must have violated every rule in the wilderness code book. To top everything, I backed into a Jumping Cholla.

The Jumping Cholla is about the spiniest cactus there is. It's full of small, chunky branches, which are covered with tiny spines. The chunks break off at the slightest contact and stay with you, causing the illusion that they've "jumped" at you from a distance. To have a behind full of cactus spines, let me tell you, is to be really in pain.

I couldn't even sit down and think things over. I took my pants off, but the trouble went deeper than that. I put my pants back on. I could have cried. And I might have if at that moment I hadn't heard the sound of a rifle.

"Hey! Hey!" I called and ran toward the sound. All of a sudden the sound of a gun seemed the most welcome sound on earth. I found them less than a quarter of a mile away.

"How come you didn't hear me call?" I said peevishly.

39

"We were in the car and had the radio on," said Cliff.

"Anyway," said Jan, "we didn't figure you'd go very far without your water canteen." There was disapproval in her voice. I told them how I'd gotten lost and admitted that I'd gone to pieces.

"Where did you grow up, kid?" Cliff said, half-joking. "Everyone knows you get a fix on where you are before you wander away from camp." Cliff showed me how to get a sense of where you are from the sun and how you can pick up clues from the land.

The slope of the barrel cactus slants toward the southwest.

Moss grows on the north side of evergreens.

The tips of evergreens generally point east.

"Or you can break a trail as you go," he said, walking along and breaking twigs as he went.

I still hadn't told Cliff and Jan about my cactus problem. But I was so uncomfortable that I couldn't let it go any longer. Neither of them laughed, which was decent.

That's my other memory of that day—me bending over in that humiliating position while Cliff pulled cactus spines out of my butt with a special tweezer that desert botanists always carry. Fortunately.

7 The Night Lizard's Babies

It wasn't until we were on the way home that night that I realized that we hadn't seen a lizard all day. With a little help from me, the conversation turned to lizards. I told Cliff about some of the lizards I'd seen since I came. And he told me a story about a lizard experience he'd had.

He'd decided to camp for a few days on a mountain in northwestern Arizona. It was a beautiful day in late October. He parked his car at the base of the mountain and began to hike up, carrying his gear and a heavier sleeping bag, because he knew it would be colder on top of the mountain.

By noon he was ready for a break. He ate his sandwich and drank his water and cussed the heavy pack. It was so hot that he considered dumping some of his gear, or hiding it under a rock and picking it up on the way down. It's a good thing he didn't.

He got to the top of the mountain about sunset. He didn't spend too much time enjoying the view, because the sun goes down pretty fast up there and he wanted to get a fire going. It was when he was collecting scrap for wood that he heard the scrambling noises in the dead yucca. Lifting a piece, he flushed out a handful of tiny, olive green, velvet-skinned lizards.

Xantusia vigilis. The Desert Night Lizard.

Cliff didn't know at the time what they were. All he knew was that they were tiny and pretty and that they were all over the place.

They're among the smallest lizards found anywhere—less than two inches long from snout to vent (the anal opening), which is the way lizards are generally measured. They live under rocks and dead vegetation, and are active during the day in spring and fall. But in summer they come out only in the cool of night.

The night lizard is one of the lizards that's gone on a different survival track. *Xantusia* has adapted to desert heat by avoiding it. In the hot weather it sleeps during the day under cool leaves and rocks. For its night prowling, it's equipped with nighttime eyes, vertical pupils that catch the maximum amount of light.

Those were the lizards that Cliff uncovered that night. They were sluggish at first. But the fire seemed to warm them up and make them more active. Two or three dashed under his shoes and one went up his pants leg. He watched them for a while and then decided to turn in.

He woke up feeling cold and wet. It was snowing.

"Feeling that snow on my face got me moving around in a hurry," Cliff told us. "It's not too healthy to be caught on top of a mountain in a blizzard when you're not prepared for it."

Cliff wasn't ready for snow. His sleeping bag was only

Desert Night Lizard

made for temperatures down to freezing, and he'd already gotten his sweater and jacket wet. It was snowing hard and it was night, so it would be difficult for him to see his way out if he decided to leave.

"As I thought about it, I wasn't in a strong position," Cliff said. "No one knew where I was, and even if they did, it would take them a good three days to get me if it snowed a lot."

He decided to look for some sort of cave to use as a shelter. He found one a little bit farther on, used his flashlight on it to make sure it wasn't already occupied by a black bear, and then moved his gear into it. When he did, one of the little lizards ran out from under his pack. On impulse, he scooped it up and put it into his pocket.

By now the temperature had gone down into the teens. Even with the little fire he'd managed to keep going on the ledge, he was plenty cold. The cave was too low for him to move around in, and just sitting made him numb.

After about an hour, Cliff decided that he'd better not try to wait out the snow. It might be a three-day blizzard. He decided to leave at daybreak.

Every once in a while he'd take the lizard out of his pocket. It was cold, so the lizard didn't do much running around. But it was something alive to keep him company. Even with the lizard, it must have been a long night. I asked him if he had been scared. He said he's a lot more scared now when he thinks about it.

"I was just uncomfortable and mad at myself because I'd gotten into such a spot. It wasn't until afterward that I thought of all the things that could have happened."

As soon as there was a little light in the sky, he started the long downward trek. Besides the fact that he had no trail to follow, he had to be very careful walking because the snow had covered the rocks and it was slippery.

"I don't think I was ever so *miserable*," he told us. "It really was hard for me to put one foot in front of the other after a while. I guess there were a few times that I thought of giving up. Once I put my hand in my pocket and felt the lizard. It was still and cold. *Almost dead*, I thought. I realized that if I'd left it there, it would have snuggled under

44

some tree trunk that was warm from rotting and been out of the elements. That reptile hadn't asked to come down the mountain. So I owed it something.

"I took the lizard out of my pocket and dropped it down the front of my shirt, right next to my body. I figured the least I could do was to share whatever body warmth I had with it."

Cliff said that all the rest of the way down he could feel the tiny creature next to his skin.

Of course, he made it. By the time he got down the mountain and into his car, the temperature on the desert was ninety degrees.

"But I couldn't stop shivering," he recalled. "I remember driving home. People were passing me, driving with their car tops down, in bathing suits. And there I was, hunched over the wheel, shivering. I shook all the way home."

I asked him what finally happened to the lizard.

Actually, that's the best part of the story. When Cliff got home, the first thing he did was to unpack the night lizard. It came around as soon as it warmed up, and Cliff put it in a tank and threw in some insects for it to eat, and let it stay there. That night it rewarded him by having two babies right in front of his eyes.

The first thing he noticed was that there was a sac protruding from the vent, which is the opening through which the lizard passes wastes and through which the female lizard is fertilized by the male. As soon as the sac was part of the way out, the mother turned around and ripped at it with her teeth until it was opened. A few minutes later a baby was born. The mother ate the sac when it had done its

45

job, and then repeated the whole process for a second off-spring. The babies immediately began crawling around like tiny copies of their mother.

I envied Cliff. He had seen something pretty rare among lizards. A live birth.

8 The Mouth of the Gila Monster

The Gila Monster may be the most misunderstood animal in existence. Take its name, for instance. Some people say Gila, in the Indian language, means spider. Of course it's not a spider. It's not a monster, either. It's simply a slow, awkward, lumbering pink-and-black lizard about sixteen to twenty inches long.

The Gila's one legitimate claim to fame is the fact that it's venomous (the only venomous lizard in the United States). But even its poison isn't rightly understood.

A woman in Ajo swore to me that she saw a Gila Monster *vomit* poison. Not true. Actually, it stores venom in glands in its jaws and releases it along grooves in its teeth when it's chewing. Maybe a long time ago the poison was a food-getting device, but now the Gila seems to use it mainly for defense. And not very often. The chances of getting bitten and *chewed* by a Gila Monster are, luckily, pretty slim. And the possibilities of dying from the bite are even smaller. All this I knew that morning in July when I found the Gila Monster.

The day was probably the hottest I had experienced in six

Gila Monster

weeks on the desert. I hadn't seen any signs of life for a few days, and I was getting fed up with everyone telling me how much more wildlife I would have seen if I'd come last year when Arizona had its usual midsummer rains.

It looked like the drought wasn't going to break at all. It was pathetic. Day after day of cloudless blue sky. In the distance the "dust devils" swirling into the air. The earth was so dry it powdered up as I walked; if I rubbed my teeth together I felt it in my mouth.

That morning at 7:45 the ground was already so hot I could feel it through my boots. I started thinking of a siesta and a shady spot. The birds seemed to have gone for good. Looking for watering places, no doubt. Some of the mammals had probably left, too. I didn't blame them. I wondered what I was doing in that dreary spot—just me and a few dried-up-looking plants. The plants had no choice, they couldn't move. But me? I could have been back at the swimming pool.

I followed the bank of the arroyo for a while, hoping for the sight of something alive. Not a chance. That place was as dead as a cemetery.

I walked around, kicking the dust and watching it sift over my boots. It seemed to me that even the bugs had deserted. And where there are no bugs there can't be lizards. Every lizard, I thought, needs insects, if not directly for food, then at least for carrying the pollen that insures a supply of plants to eat. No bugs, no lizards.

Suddenly I came on a pack-rat hole. I poked around inside it, using my stick as a probe. Pack rats are interesting. They make their nests of assorted junk and are sometimes

49

attracted to beer-can tabs and other unlikely bedding material. I was poking around and grinning at all the crazy things the pack rat had collected when I saw it—the Gila Monster.

It was sleeping. Or maybe *estivating*, which is a kind of hibernation which certain animals go into during periods of heat and drought. When reptiles go into this state all their body functions slow down and they don't have to eat or drink because they're not using any energy.

So there was the Gila Monster, maybe with all its systems turned almost all the way off. And here I was, disturbing it.

It stirred. I went a few feet away and sat down on a rock, torn between wanting to leave it alone and wanting to see it in action. I finally decided to see if I could find it some food and put it right in front of the nest. Maybe the smell would awaken it and I could watch it eat.

There were a couple of things wrong with that idea, as I think about it now. Gila Monsters don't smell things in the same way that we do. They rely mostly on their tongues. The lizard would have had to flick out its tongue to sample the air and then carry the chemical particles back to a scent organ located in the roof of its mouth. But why would it awaken and flick its tongue out in the first place?

The second problem was where I was going to get food. Gila Monsters normally live on birds' eggs and young hatchling birds. The chances of my finding a bird egg at this time of year were practically zero.

Then I remembered my lunch. Hard-boiled eggs. Maybe it wouldn't eat the egg hard-boiled. But it was worth a try.

50

I took an egg from my pack and laid it on the sand. Then I picked up my stick and tried to poke the lizard awake. I couldn't raise it at all. I really wanted to reach in with my hand, pull it out, and hold it for inspection. But I was afraid to.

So there I sat, on my rock, pondering the situation. I had seen a Gila but I hadn't really seen it. A sleeping Gila Monster is not your most dynamic experience.

Just then I heard some rustling from inside the nest. I got down on my knees and peered in. It was moving!

I thought, wrongly as it turned out, that somehow it had gotten wind of my egg. But I didn't want it to be scared by my presence. So I waited quietly on my rock. In a few minutes it came out of the pack-rat nest.

I can't say that Gila Monster was a great-looking specimen. It looked as wrinkled and dried out as everything else on the desert. Its tail, which should have been round and fat, was as skinny as an old rope. Some lizards live off the fat in their tails when food-getting is hard.

Now it was out of the burrow. I expected it to move toward my egg. Instead, it moved slowly in the opposite direction, in a purposeful way. I followed, keeping a respectable distance. Now its tongue was flicking in and out of its mouth. In a few minutes I saw why. A tiny Zebra-tailed Lizard, on its back in the sun.

Dead.

I could see a flurry of scratch marks around the site. As if it had tried desperately to bury itself before it had been struck down. But the sand in this spot was baked hard as a rock.

Maybe it had been overcome by an internal parasite. It was hard to know. Whatever had happened must have just happened, because some other creature would have eaten it if it had been there for any length of time. As it was, it had already attracted the ants. So much for my idea that there were no insects around.

The Gila Monster certainly was not concerned with what had happened to the Zebra-tailed Lizard. It was concerned simply with satisfying its appetite.

Ordinarily, Gila Monsters do not eat lizards. They're not fast enough to catch most day lizards. So this was probably a special meal.

I watched it bite into the meat, oblivious to the ants. I wondered if as it chewed, venom was running into that already dead lizard. *Overkill*, I thought.

I took my other egg out of the pack and ate and drank as I watched the Gila Monster. I imagined a conversation that tickled me.

"What did you do today?"

"Oh, I had lunch with a Gila Monster."

"What did you have?"

"Oh, I had eggs and a ham-and-lettuce sandwich. He had lizard."

It was time to look for shade. I scouted the bank of the wash for a tree that would give me some and still put me near the Gila Monster. As I was doing that I happened to glance up. Away in the distance there was a faint haze. Not smog. No! Rain! It was raining up in the mountains. Once my attention was on it, I noticed the darker color of the sky in the mountain area. And then I heard the thunder.

Rain at last! But the mountains get more condensation

anyway. They don't need it like we need it down here. Let them have it. I checked the Gila Monster. Still eating.

Sun high. *Hot.* Siesta time.

The Gila Monster agreed. It finished its meal and wandered back to the rat nest. Obviously had some sense of direction.

I picked my tree. Ironwood. Nice big one. I spread a tarp on the branches and another on the ground and used my pack for a pillow.

"What did you do after lunch?"

"Oh, took a nap. So did the Gila Monster."

I slept. About half an hour later I was awakened by a noise. Kind of a rumbling. I looked around, but I couldn't see anything. I did notice, though, that the sun had gone in and there was a definite breeze.

The rumbling got louder.

Now the sky was definitely overcast. I wondered if it was possible that we were going to get some rain after all. I scanned the sky. I also began to look around for possible shelter in case of a storm.

Now the noise that I'd been hearing was too loud and close to be ignored. It was definitely coming from the direction of the mountains and it was definitely something important. Five minutes later I saw what it was.

A flash flood.

I'd read about them, but now I was actually seeing one. It was a half hour since I'd heard and seen the first signs of the storm. And now it was coming at me. I was about to be engulfed by the most torrential body of water I'd ever seen outside of the Atlantic Ocean.

It was still some distance away. I scrambled for higher

ground, barely getting my pack. I left my tarp hanging on the tree. I *moved*. I knew that water was going to come right down the arroyo.

Two minutes later it was swirling past me, muddy and mean, sweeping away everything in its path. I saw the pack-rat house go. I strained my eyes looking for the Gila Monster.

Had it left while I was asleep? Or was it swirling down in that torrent toward the plain where this water would eventually wind up and evaporate, and where all the dead creatures would be food for the live ones?

Maybe it got away, I told myself. Maybe that's what woke it up. Some instinct had warned it of the storm. That wasn't such a far-out idea. Lizards' bodies are very sensitive to changes in the barometric pressure. I hoped the Gila's barometer had been working overtime.

I watched a bird's nest spin by. Now the thunderheads had developed over where I was. It was getting darker and the wind was blowing the dried weed around. I figured my sister would leave work and come get me if she knew it was storming out here. But she might not know. It might be clear where she was.

It started to rain. I smelled that smell of water mixing with dry ground. It rained. It poured. The water pelted down and it was as black as midnight and the wind came up and tore the words out of my mouth as I hollered. Who was I hollering to? I don't know.

I saw my tarp go flying off the ironwood tree into the water. I held on to my pack, finally putting it on top of my head as a shield. Now hailstones were coming down, as big as golf balls. How weird it would be to be knocked cold by a piece of ice.

There was no shelter for me anywhere. No house, no lean-to. It was out of the question to walk to the road and hope to hitch a ride.

I sat still and let the rain pelt me. At least I was cool. Then, as quickly as it had come, it suddenly let up.

The sun came out.

The only signs of the storm were the little puddles of water in the depressions in the earth. That, and the water still tumbling down the arroyo.

I walked over there carefully. I wasn't anxious to get too close and have the soil give way on the bank. That water still looked fierce. I debated following it downstream to see if I could get my tarp back. I decided against it.

The sun was just as hot as it was before. The ground was drying at an incredible rate. So were my clothes. I figured that by the time Jan came to pick me up, she'd never know that I had been caught in a storm unless I told her.

I started to walk around a big puddle. And there was the Gila Monster! Giving itself a good soaking. In no hurry to leave. When a Gila Monster can get water, it hangs around.

Stay, I urged the Gila Monster. *Relax. Enjoy.*

The Gila Monster stayed in its bath for about forty minutes. Then, at 6:03 P.M., it walked off in a westerly direction with the sun on its back and the shadows doing funny things to its colors. In a few minutes, I'd lost it.

9 The Rattle of the Snake

At dusk the animals that have been active during the day disappear. The night shift begins to take over the desert.

I remember one particular night. We were driving along a blacktop road, hoping to see some nocturnal lizards. But that night was snake night. I think I saw more snakes on the road that night than I've ever seen at one time in my whole life.

Of course there's nothing odd about seeing snakes on the road at night. Any snake collector will tell you that's the time to look for them. Snakes like to crawl on warm blacktop when the night air begins to cool the desert floor. It's a way to keep your belly warm if you're a reptile.

At 7:05 we spotted the first one. It was tiny, only about ten inches long. We thought it was a piece of rope until we slowed down and saw it moving. I got out of the car and identified it as a Western Blind Snake. Not such a hard identification—blind snakes have little eye spots on their heads which seem to mimic eyes.

It's rare to see a blind snake. They spend a lot of time

underground. In fact, scientists think that all snakes may be branches of a group of lizards that began to live underground as a result of some change in climate topside. It's pretty certain that snakes once had legs and then, after a time, evolved legless because of their underground life. One of the evidences for this is that some snakes still have a small spur, or leg, that is a "leftover" from that time.

I wondered whether blind snakes became blind because they stayed underground, or whether they stay underground because they're blind.

In any case, that snake wasn't safe on the highway. I picked it up and put it in the underbrush at the side of the road. I made an entry about it in my notebook.

Fifteen minutes later, passing through a rocky canyon slope, we found a Rosy Boa. That's a beautiful snake. This one was pinkish with brown stripes. We stopped again and moved it off the road. I had half a mind to keep that snake, but Jan persuaded me not to. Let it stay wild, she advised. She was right.

A little after seven-thirty, we found what was left of a bull snake that had been hit by a car. Out came the notebook again. 7:35 P.M., bull snake, forty inches, D.O.R. (dead on road).

At 8:05 we saw the biggest Western Diamondback Rattlesnake either of us had ever seen. By that time it was beginning to get dark, but even in failing light there was no mistaking the banded black-and-white tail and the splotchy tan body. The snake was over six feet long. I had visions of that rattler in a couple of years stretching from one side of the blacktop road clear across to the other.

It was taking its sweet time crossing, and it didn't seem to mind our presence. It slithered along with graceful snaky ease. It looked so innocent, so harmless. When you see a poisonous snake with plenty of space around it for you and it, it's hard to believe that it's dangerous.

But Jan and I both knew it was. There was probably enough venom in that snake's jaws to kill both of us, although that's not its purpose. Actually, venom is just a way for the snake to catch its prey—the "gun" of the hunter snake, you might say. Rattlers bite people only as a defense.

Western Diamondback Rattlesnake

So we kept our distance. Snakebite was not on my schedule of events for that vacation.

I looked at the rattler's tail. It had a fine string of rattles; there looked to be ten or more. The rattle of a rattlesnake is really an odd mechanism. I read somewhere that the rattling sound that comes from a rattlesnake's tail is made by the segments rubbing together. And that a rattler can shake its tail so that they touch as much as a thousand times a second!

I thought we should do something to get the Diamondback off the road. Jan balked at first. But I gave her my big lecture about how if we didn't it might get hit by a car and about how all snakes help the balance of nature. I stressed the fact that snakes eat mice and rats which destroy crops and *plants*. The way to Jan's heart is through her green thumb.

So she agreed, somewhat reluctantly, to help. I found two big Saguaro ribs and gave her one. Together we half-pushed and half-lifted the snake into the underbrush on the side of the road. We were careful to stay away from the head. Even so, the rattler didn't appreciate the free ride at all. It set up such a buzzing in that tail we figured they could hear it back in Phoenix.

Jan hated the sound. "It's downright menacing," she said. "No wonder people are afraid of snakes."

I explained to Jan that the rattling wasn't anything the snake thought about. It was simply a reflex. And a mixed blessing for the snake. It sometimes draws attention to itself at times when it would be better off leaving quietly. In a world where rattling scares your enemies, it's good to

59

have it. But where people who hate snakes have guns, it might be better to just slip away without being seen or heard.

In some parts of the United States, rattlers seem to be evolving without rattles. A clear case of evolution working for the survival of the species.

10 The Eye of the Gecko

Just as it got dark, we came to an old shack. There aren't many houses in that part of the desert, so we decided to investigate. We got out of The Heap with our lanterns and tramped across the sand. No sign of life inside the house. But the door was open. And there was something carved in the lintel above the doorway. *Eighteen-sixty-two.* Jan told me that was the year of the Homestead Act, when the government passed a law giving people land in the West if they'd go out and settle on it. A lot of people went. Somebody must have staked a claim to that piece of desert, once, and built the house.

We shone our lights around inside. Not much of a house. And it stank of sheep. Someone had been using it for a sheep pen. Indian sheepherders, probably. The smell was too much for Jan. She said she'd wait for me outside.

I held my light up so I could see better. There was a kind of crude shelf along one wall of the cabin and an old wooden crate standing in the middle of the room.

Nothing else, unless you want to count the hay and the sheep dung in the corner.

The corner. That's where the lizard was. It must have seen me before I saw it. It moved to hide and that was the little scrambling sound I heard. I peered into the corner and saw two tiny spots of eyeshine and a little shape.

I moved fast. I grabbed the wooden box and dropped the open end over where the shape was. Everything was quiet for a minute. Then a thin squeaking sound began to come from under the box. The lizard was actually making a noise!

As soon as I heard that sound, I knew I'd caught myself a gecko.

I stood for a minute, enjoying the capture. Then I carefully pried up one of the slats at the top of the box with my penknife and shone my light inside.

The gecko was looking up at me, standing stiff-legged, all three inches of it a challenge—poised to do battle with me. I felt like Gulliver in the land of the Lilliputians. Poor little thing, bobbing its head at me in what was supposed to be a threatening way. I put my hand down into the box.

First the gecko ran into a corner. When I followed it with my hand, it turned around and tried to bite me. It really wasn't a fair contest. I ran my hand around the box, pinned the gecko against the side, and then lifted it out.

This time I was careful not to grab the tail. I held its body until I could work the neck between my fingers lightly in the way that the field guide recommends. It was only after I was holding it that I saw that my specimen had two tails! Geckos are known as tail-droppers, and this Desert Banded Gecko had once lost its tail and was growing back *two* new ones. That made it rather special. I decided to keep it for a while.

62

I brought it outside and showed Jan, and she agreed that a lizard with two tails was worth keeping. So we brought it home with us and put it in one of the fish tanks, which I filled with sand.

The next day I had a chance to get a good look at it. It was the most delicate lizard I'd seen so far. Its skin looked more like velvet than scales, and it was so thin you could see the pulsing and the shape of its organs through the skin.

Jan really liked the gecko. She was fascinated by its dappled yellow-and-brown color and its huge eyes. "Pip," she said. "It has eyes. It's *winking*!"

The eyes had it for me, too. I decided to find out more about them. I discovered some good gecko-eye information

Desert Banded Gecko

in a book called *Desert: The American Southwest,* by Ruth Kirk. Kirk says that the eyes of geckos are designed to catch every bit of night light. The retina is outfitted like a reflecting mirror in a camera. The eye receives incoming light *twice*—once when the light comes in and again almost at the same time when it bounces off the "mirror." It's this "mirror" that makes nocturnal animals' eyes shine. The pupil of the gecko's eye is even more spectacular. In the human eye, the pupil simply gets smaller and larger depending on how much light enters. But in a night animal like the gecko, too much bright daylight could be bad for an eye used to darkness. So for protection, the gecko has vertical slits that can be widened or narrowed, like sunshades, to let in more or less light. And it has little notches alongside the slits to let in pinholes of light without letting in glare.

As much as we liked Bright Eyes, he didn't seem to return our affection. He kept trying to hide. I put a few rocks in the tank to give him a cave, and he ran in there and hid for the rest of the day.

I had already noticed that he had two well-developed anal spurs, one on each side of his tail. So he was a male.

The next night I fed him some live flies and spiders that I had collected. He ate each one the same way—a twitch of the tail, a lunge, and he'd have it. Then would come the chewing and the swallowing. And after he'd finished swallowing, he'd lick his jaws with his tongue, like a kid who's just finished a piece of candy. I never got tired of watching him eat. I bet Jan that I'd have him eating out of my hand in a week.

64

We'd had him about four days when one evening I arrived at the tank just in time to get a demonstration of how *Coleonyx variegatus* sheds its skin. When I got there the old skin was already off his back, but there was still some on his feet. He began to pull it off with his mouth just as if he were taking off a glove. He didn't stop until all the old skin was off all twenty toes. Then he ate it. "Talk about recycling!" Jan commented.

After he'd shed, the gecko looked particularly bright. Reptiles always look brighter after they shed. But I suspected that it was also because it was breeding time for geckos, and one of the ways the males attract the females is by color.

It may have been breeding time that was responsible for our losing Bright Eyes. One night he found a way out of the tank. When we looked for him the next morning he was gone.

I hope he got out to the desert, to call and chirp, and to look for a female with his big bright eyes. I hope he found her. I hope they bobbed heads at each other and waved their tails at each other, the way courting geckos do.

I hope they mated. Because if they did, later in the summer she laid two soft-shelled eggs. And if all went well, they hatched in the fall.

By this time the offspring of Bright Eyes may be scurrying around looking for *their* mates somewhere near that round house in the desert.

11 The Heat of the Desert

August in Gila Bend and Lukeville and Yuma. Not to be believed. See life through a haze of heat. Breathe and feel hot air coming into your lungs. Step out of your air-conditioned house into an oven.

"Sure you want to do this?" Jan asked me for the fourth time. *This* was to be dropped off in a stretch of desert near the Mexican border to look for Chuckwalla lizards in the lava rock. Not only was I going to be dropped off, I was to be left overnight.

I considered this trip my farewell to the desert. I was going home at the end of the week, and this was the first and last time I'd be camping overnight alone.

I was a little nervous. There was something about the heat and the moonscape of southwestern Arizona that was getting to me. Besides, we'd heard a story the previous night that didn't do much for my jitters. A few days before we'd arrived, two teenagers had gone out on the missile range to get shell casings. A buddy waiting for them in a car was spotted by an Army patrol and he took off, leaving the kids to fend for themselves without water. They panicked. They hid under the trees so the helicopters couldn't find them. They took all their clothes off and ran around until they were exhausted and dehydrated. The helicopters found them two days later—dead.

So I felt creepy. But when Jan asked me if I wanted to change my mind, I shook my head and said no, that I'd be fine.

I had supplies enough for a week. And if advice can be counted a supply, I was stocked up for a month. I had my canteen, a ten-gallon tank of water, and a bottle of salt tablets. I also had a tent, a cot, blankets, matches, a light, and enough food for an army.

But the water was the important thing. It used to seem silly to me that so much fuss is made about drinking water in the desert. If you're not thirsty, it's hard to imagine craving a drink all that much. But the fact is, *nobody* can live for more than a day in the desert without water.

The kangaroo rat can live almost entirely without drinking water because it gets the liquid it needs from its food. The Desert Tortoise can make do with very little water, too. The horned lizard gets its liquid from ants and the Desert Iguana gets most of its from plants.

But desert animals, like many animals, don't *sweat*. A person can sweat as much as a half gallon of water an hour in the desert. And that water has to be replaced if the person is to survive.

I waved Jan good-bye, and as I watched the good old Heap bumping along the sand, I couldn't help thinking,

Arizona Chuckwalla

Here I am about to spend a day and night in a place lizards are a lot more fit to live in than I am.

I spent some time setting up the tent and the cot and getting the food and water inside. I'd picked a spot on the western side of a lava rock wall, so that when the sun began to go down, the rocks would cast some shadow on the tent and make it cooler. Saving even that much "cool" is to be desired; it might mean several degrees, and I was glad that I'd thought of it.

I set up a cot and put my sleeping bag on it. Sleeping on the ground, say the desert buffs, makes you the warm body that a snake can snuggle up to in the dark.

By the time I finished setting up, I was hungry and thirsty. I had a tuna-fish sandwich (salty food makes you drink), a lot of water, and a Survival Brownie.

Survival Brownies are Jan's invention. She makes them by spreading granola cereal on a cookie sheet, adding a little honey, baking it awhile, and then cutting it into bars. She claims a person could live on Survival Brownies and water.

When I came out of the tent the sun was dazzling. I put on my sunglasses and waited for those red whirling things to stop dancing in front of my eyes. Then I began to look around.

I'll never forget that afternoon on the desert. There wasn't a sound. Not a buzzing, croaking, cheeping, chirping, hissing, scrambling sound. I would have welcomed the buzzing of a rattlesnake, I think. The longer it went on, the lonelier I felt. Like an astronaut on some new planet, exploring all by himself.

69

I found myself thinking of reasons to go back to the tent every few minutes and survey the familiar objects. Bed. Food. Shelter. I rested often, kept my hat on, and drank what seemed an enormous quantity of water. About two-thirty, I began to seriously look for Chuckwallas.

The Chuckwalla is a big, slow, blackish, mottled lizard. *Sauromalus obesus. Sauromalus* means bad lizard. *Obesus* means fat. It's generally found on rocks. It lives in rock crevices from which it comes out to spend long hours basking in the sun at temperatures which could kill a person, and which drive other lizards back into their holes. Its color varies with its age, sex, and locality. Chuckwallas tend to match the color of the rocks they live on.

At 3:10, I spotted two blue gray Chuckwallas in the blue gray lava rock about twenty-five feet from the place where my tent was. Mother and offspring? I wondered. Or male and female? The female Chuckwalla has a banded tail. So do the young. One of these two had a banded tail.

I heard a funny scraping sound. It seemed very loud because it was so quiet there. It was another Chuckwalla moving into place on the rock. Its thick, scaly skin rasped along the rock. Soon there were five of them, sitting up there in their dragon costumes, sunning.

I was full of self-praise. How clever of me to have spotted the little pill-shaped droppings that marked their hideout. I moved far enough away so as not to scare them, and watched them through the glasses. After a few minutes I moved forward and they vanished into crevices in the rock.

I was a little leery about climbing up to the ledge and poking around in there. It looked like rattlesnake territory

—lots of dark shelves of rock. But I was careful where I stepped and made sure that I didn't put my hands too close to those openings in the rock. I made my way over to where the Chucks were. I took a stick and began to poke down the hole where I'd seen them disappear.

Chuckwallas have a neat defense when they're trapped in their rock fortresses. They suck in air and inflate their bodies like balloons until they're so tightly wedged that nothing will budge them.

That's what they were doing. I could see one of them down there, all puffed up. But I kept at it, hoping I could get it to back out of the other side of the opening.

I remembered a story I'd read about Chuckwallas being hunted this way for food. The Indians would hunt a Chuck into its hole and then deflate it by ramming a stick into the lizard's gut.

They're supposed to taste like chicken. Everything's supposed to taste like chicken—frog, snake, iguana. I don't like chicken.

I thought of a way to get the Chuckwalla out. I pried up the top rock with one end of my lizard noose, which took the roof off the Chuckwalla's house. I was surprised when I got a look down to see that there were three of them in one crevice. I reached down and pulled one out. It bit me, but I held on anyway.

The bite didn't break the skin. I got a better grip and held the Chuckwalla so the tail couldn't do me any damage.

With the Chuck immobilized, I was able to measure it. It was eighteen inches long, counting its tail. One big lizard! The banded tail marked it for a female. I wondered if she was about to lay eggs. I wondered how old she was, when she had last eaten, and why Chuckwallas eat flowers and leaves instead of insects.

One thing I didn't have to wonder about—her mood. That lizard was mad! She thrashed around so much I could hardly hold her. Rather than aggravate her further, I put her back in her hole and replaced the top rock. I could hear her scrambling away to a deeper and safer place.

It's amazing how tired that little bit of activity made me. I went back to the tent, drank about a gallon of water, and had two salt tablets. The truth is, you really can't *do* much on a hot day in the desert. Siesta time, I thought gratefully, stretching out on my cot.

12 The Sting of the Scorpion

That night I made a fire and had a good meal and turned in early. I lay awake for a while, hearing the little scrabbly sounds of small night creatures around the tent, but I wasn't afraid. The night somehow seemed less threatening than the day.

I was up really early the next morning. It was still cool, and I was anxious to do some exploring before the heat of the day was on me. My shirt felt pretty raunchy after I'd worn it a whole day and then slept in it. I decided to change. I pulled another shirt out of my pack and was buttoning it when I felt a sharp pain in the back of my neck. I yelled, and slapped at the spot. My hand touched something hard and big.

It was a scorpion.

I knew only enough about scorpions to remember that their sting ranges from mildly uncomfortable to deadly. That was just enough information to panic me.

Jan and I had been careful. We had provided protection against heat, cold, thirst, hunger—we had even packed a snakebite kit. But this—this was the unexpected. And the terrifying.

It was my own fault. Good camping practice, particularly in the desert, requires that you always shake out the bedding before lying down, and shake out the clothes before putting them on. The reason? Scorpions, centipedes, and two species of poisonous spiders.

I had forgotten. I had also forgotten that many more people in the United States die from venomous insect and arachnid bites than they do from reptile bites. That was not a particularly comforting statistic for me at that moment.

I was definitely bitten. The dead scorpion lay in my palm. It was big and tan. Its stinger was clearly visible. The question was—was it one of the more venomous species? Would I get mild swelling and discomfort, or would I be one of those fatality statistics? I seemed to remember something about the bite swelling if it wasn't venomous and not swelling if it was. Or was it the other way around?

I put my hand to my neck. It was definitely swelling. And painful. Hot to the touch. My head throbbed. The neck, I thought, is too close to the brain. I could become paralyzed.

I wish I could say I was brave and calm, but I wasn't. I grabbed my canteen and began pouring water over my head like a maniac.

I managed to waste two quarts of water before I realized how foolish I was acting. I re-capped the canteen carefully after I wet a rag with water and slapped it on my neck. That sobered me a little. I sat down to try to make some decisions.

If the scorpion bite was venomous I should get to a

doctor. So, therefore, I should try to make it to the road and hope for a passing car to stop for me.

But if I tried to make it to the road . . . that was seven miles and I'd have to do it by compass. And all deserts look alike . . . and I was woozy and had a terrible headache. What shape would I be in by high noon?

When I realized that I'd have to limit myself to two quarts of water because I couldn't carry any more, I decided to stay put. By that time I had myself under a little better control. My head still ached, but not unbearably, and the fire in my neck was cooling down.

I had seven hours to kill before Jan would arrive, so I decided the best thing to do was to take it easy. I lay down

Giant Hairy Scorpion

on the cot, tried to relax, and went over the events of the last hour.

Funny the way things happen. I'd had a feeling all along that this particular day had some kind of hex on it. But I'd been looking for the trouble in the wrong direction.

I thought my problem would be water. So I'd rehearsed in my mind a hundred ways to survive in the desert if your water supply goes:

> *Drink the inside of the barrel cactus.*
> *Chew edible leaves.*
> *Watch where the birds go and follow them to the water holes.*

Make a desert still—that was my favorite. You can actually build a small water condenser with a piece of plastic, a can, and a shovel. You dig a funnel-like hole, line it with cactus stems, and cover it with plastic. You put the can at the bottom of the hole. After a while, the water condenses on the plastic and runs down into the can. That was my most sophisticated piece of survival knowledge.

I had even made a desert still in the backyard of Jan's house. A lot of good it had done me. I had prepared for the wrong emergency, I thought bitterly.

I was still feeling dizzy. I drank some water and lay down again. I knew now I had to stay put. Five hours to go before Jan would come.

Indian yogis can slow down their breathing and their heartbeat. So can lizards.

Why was I sweating so much? And drinking so much water? And then losing it by sweating and urinating so much?

76

Lizards don't sweat. They don't have to have so much water. They don't even lose much water when they urinate.

I re-wet the rag and put it on my head.

God, it was so *hot*!

As soon as there was some shade I decided to move my tent to another spot where the lava wall cast more of a shadow. I figured when I was done that the amount of body energy I used up in the moving about equaled the additional cool I got from it. That's the way I was beginning to think. I was having my own personal energy crisis.

What if Jan got delayed? She wouldn't rush because she didn't know I was in trouble. The thought made me so nervous I had to pee again.

Now I was beginning to get nauseous. I was sure I had a fever. I drifted off to sleep in that soundless void.

I'll never forget the dream I had that afternoon. In it, I was both lying on my cot and standing watching myself. The tent had disappeared and I was a small figure lying on a cot in the midst of an enormous sandy plain. There was nothing as far as the eye could see except the lizards scurrying over the desert floor. They passed my cot in a hurried parade—the whiptails and geckos, the Gila Monsters and horned lizards, the iguanas—all the lizards I had seen on the desert.

I was unable to move to chase them—nor was the figure on the cot able to move. I stood and watched and lay staring up at a cloudless sky, through which the vultures moved, circling circling. . . .

I awakened to the sound of The Heap. I stood up and promptly fainted.

By the next day I was fine. Jan said I'd been bitten by

the Giant Hairy Scorpion, which, luckily, is not one of the lethal varieties. I'd been stricken as much by fear and heat as by the sting of the scorpion, we decided. I left for home that morning with a stiff neck and a fever sore. Jan felt terrible sending me home in that shape. But I assured her I was fine and that I'd had a great time. A real adventure.

I left that marvelous adobe house for the last time. The sun was just coming up over the desert. The birds were already busy at the front-yard feeder. As The Heap pulled out of the driveway, a family of Gambel's Quail crossed the road. The "boss" quail chattered a warning and the young scurried frantically into the bush.

And then the desert was quiet. But I knew that somewhere out there—under the creosote bushes and the prickly pear cacti and the ocotillo and yucca—somewhere the diurnal lizards were stirring. As they had done for millions of years before I came to watch them. As they would do for millions of years after I was gone.

Bibliography

Books About Deserts

Abbey, Edward, and the editors of *Life, Cactus Country.* New York: Time Inc., 1973.

Adolph, Edward Frederick, and others, *Physiology of Man in the Desert.* New York: Hafner Press, 1969.

Brown, George Willard, ed., *Desert Biology.* New York: Academic Press, Inc., 1968.

Cloudsley-Thompson, J.L., and Chadwick, N.J., *Life in Deserts.* Chester Springs, Pa.: Dufour Editions, Inc., 1964.

Costello, David Francis, *The Desert World.* New York: T. Y. Crowell Co., 1972.

Hastings, James R., and Turner, Raymond, *The Changing Mile.* Tucson: University of Arizona Press, 1965.

Jaeger, Edmund Carroll, *Desert Wildlife.* Stanford: Stanford University Press, 1961.

Jaeger, Edmund Carroll, *The North American Deserts.* Stanford: Stanford University Press, 1957.

Kirk, Ruth, *Desert: The American Southwest.* Boston: Houghton Mifflin Company, 1973.

Krutch, Joseph Wood, *The Voice of the Desert*. New York: William Morrow & Co., Inc., 1955.

Larson, Peggy, *Deserts of America*. Englewood Cliffs, N. J.: Prentice-Hall, Inc., 1970.

Schmidt-Neilsen, Knut, *Desert Animals: Physiological Problems of Heat and Water*. New York: Oxford University Press, Inc., 1964.

Sutton, Ann, and Sutton, Myron, *Life of the Desert*. New York: McGraw-Hill, Inc., 1966.

Woodin, Ann, *Home Is the Desert*. New York: The Macmillan Company, 1970.

Books About Lizards

Carr, Archie, and the editors of *Life*, *The Reptiles*. New York: Time, Inc., 1968.

D'a Bellairs, Angus, *The Life of Reptiles*, Vols. I & II. New York: Universe Books, 1970.

Gans, Carl, *Biology of the Reptilia*. New York: Academic Press, Inc., 1970.

Inger, Robert F., Schmidt, Karl Patterson, *Living Reptiles of the World*. Garden City, N. Y.: Doubleday & Company, Inc., 1957.

Leviton, Alan E., *Reptiles and Amphibians of North America*. Garden City, N. Y.: Doubleday & Company, Inc., 1972.

Milstead, William W., editor, *Lizard Ecology: A Symposium*. Columbia, Mo.: University of Missouri Press, 1965.

Porter, Kenneth R., *Herpetology*. Philadelphia: W.B. Saunders Company, 1972.

Richardson, Maurice, *The Fascination of Reptiles*. New York: Hill and Wang, 1972.

Smith, Hobart Muir, *Handbook of Lizards: Lizards of the United States and Canada*. Sausalito, Cal.: Comstock Editions, 1946.

Index

82

83

Format by Joyce Hopkins
Set in 11 pt. Primer
Composed by The Haddon Craftsmen, Inc.
Printed by The Murray Printing Company
Bound by The Haddon Craftsmen, Inc.
HARPER & ROW, PUBLISHERS, INCORPORATED